Night Night, Curiosity

Brianna Caplan Sayres

Illustrated by Ryan O'Rourke

ini Charlesbridge

Dad flies me
up the stairway. . . .

I'm blasting off for Mars.
Beside me is a rover.
We hurtle toward the stars!

Dad whisks me down the hallway. . . .

It's a vast and empty place.
For months and months we travel.
Our rocket speeds through space.

Dad wraps me in a towel. . . .

Our journey's quite a feat.
We hit the Martian atmosphere.
Our shield burns bright with heat.

We cuddle with
my bedtime book. . . .

We're racing toward the sand.
Our parachute helps slow us down.
It's time for us to land.

Dad lifts me
to my bed. . . .

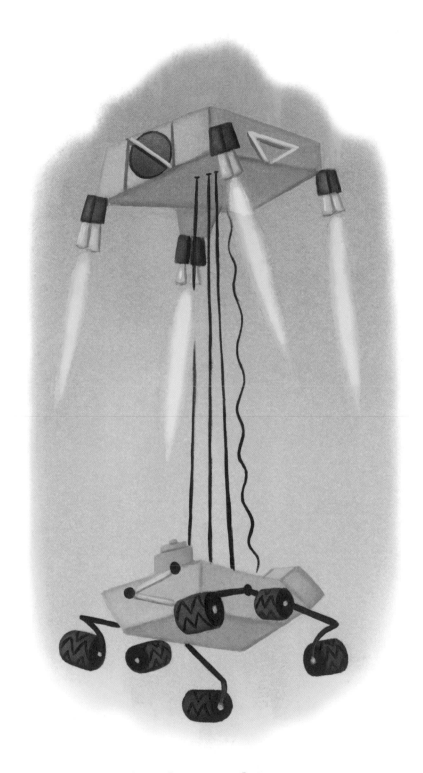

We mustn't kick up dust.
We're lowered by a sky crane. . . .

Will our plan work out? It must!

I beg for one more story. . . .

Back home on Earth they wait.
Then they get the signal
that they can celebrate.

I'm cozy in my blankets. . . .

Then a message—loud and clear.
Our antenna soon receives the voice
I really want to hear.

Mom calls from work
to say good night. . . .

We'll send these pictures home.

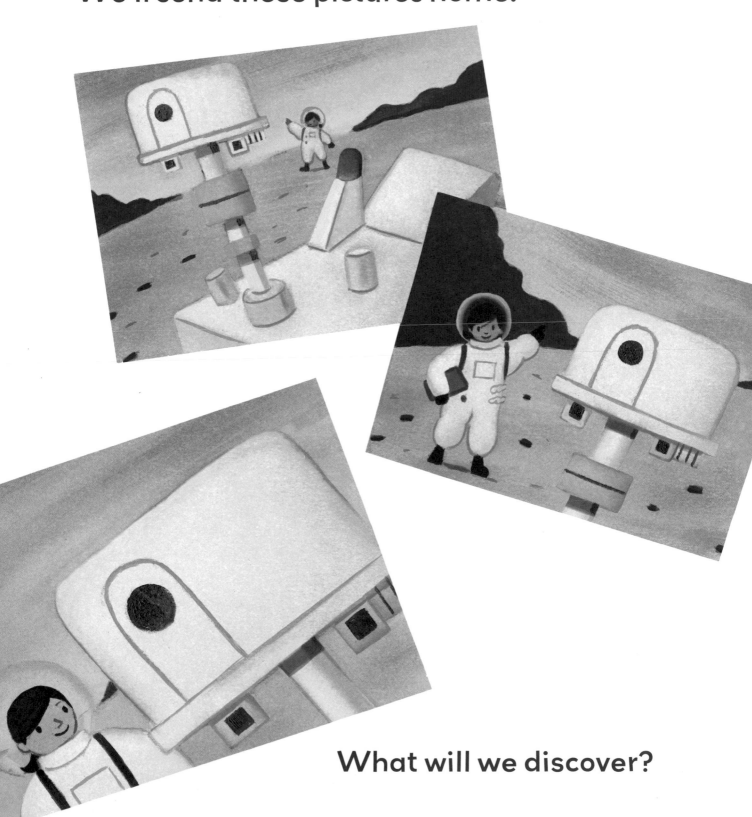

What will we discover?

What places will we roam?

On Mars I start to yawn.
Exploring this red planet
will have to wait till dawn.

Dad tucks me in and hugs me. . . .

The day turns into night.
I gaze at Mars's mountains.
What an awe-inspiring sight!

Dad gives me
one more kiss
and hug. . . .

I catch a glimpse of light.
"Night night, Curiosity!"

"Night night!"

Curiosity, a car-sized rover, landed on Mars on August 5, 2012. It took 253 days for the rover to reach Mars from Earth. Finally Mission Control got word that *Curiosity* had started to descend. For seven scary minutes, they waited. Until . . . "Touchdown confirmed." *Curiosity* was safely on Mars. This remarkable landing included all the steps that the girl in this book imagines. *Curiosity*'s mission is to discover whether Mars is or ever was a planet that could support life. *Curiosity* drills into rocks, studies dirt samples, and sends back pictures of Mars (including selfies!). After all these years, *Curiosity* is still going strong, exploring and making discoveries about the red planet.

Acknowledgments

With thanks to Dr. Sarah Milkovich, planetary geologist and science systems engineer at NASA Jet Propulsion Laboratory, California Institute of Technology. Thank you so very much for asking for this bedtime book and for checking it for accuracy. And with thanks to Teresa Kietlinski, my out-of-this-world agent. Thank you so much for your incredible idea for Mom.

For Carl, who always encourages me to reach for the stars!—B. C. S.

For Kaylee, Riley, and Liam—R. O.

Published by Charlesbridge
9 Galen Street, Watertown, MA 02472
(617) 926-0329 • www.charlesbridge.com

Printed in China
(hc) 10 9 8 7 6 5 4 3 2 1

Illustrations done in digital mixed media
Display type hand-lettered by Ryan O'Rourke
Text type set in Grenadine MVB by Markanna Studios Inc.
Color separations by Colourscan Print Co Pte Ltd, Singapore
Printed by 1010 Printing International Limited in Huizhou, Guangdong, China
Production supervision by Brian G. Walker
Designed by Sarah Richards Taylor and Jon Simeon

Library of Congress Cataloging-in-Publication Data
Names: Sayres, Brianna Caplan, author. |
    O'Rourke, Ryan, illustrator.
Title: Night night, Curiosity / Brianna Caplan Sayres;
    illustrated by Ryan O'Rourke.
Description: Watertown, MA: Charlesbridge, [2020] |
Summary: Told in rhyming text, a young girl imagines
    herself on a mission to Mars with Curiosity, the
    Mars rover, as she gets ready to go to bed.
Identifiers: LCCN 2018058511 (print) |
    LCCN 2018060773 (ebook) |
    ISBN 9781632897626 (ebook) |
    ISBN 9781580898935 (reinforced for library use)
Subjects: LCSH: Curiosity (Spacecraft)—
    Juvenile fiction. | Imagination—Juvenile fiction. |
    Bedtime—Juvenile fiction. | Stories in rhyme. |
    Mars (Planet)—Exploration—Juvenile fiction. |
    CYAC: Stories in rhyme. | Curiosity (Spacecraft)—
    Fiction. | Imagination—Fiction. | Bedtime—
    Fiction. | Mars (Planet)—Exploration—Fiction. |
    LCGFT: Stories in rhyme.
Classification: LCC PZ8.3.S274 (ebook) | LCC PZ8.3.S274
    Ni 2020 (print) | DDC [E]—dc23
LC record available at https://lccn.loc.gov/2018058511